FROM DINOSAUR TO DINOSTAR
PARASAUROLOPHUS

ROLO (Parasaurolophus)

Scientist and cleverest of the Dinostars. She is usually found in her lab conducting experiments.

- Favourite colour: **Yellow**
- Favourite subject: **Quantum Physics**
- Languages spoken: **37 (including Martian Tongue-Clicking and Dino-Roaring)**
- Did you know?
  She has an IQ of 300 and can complete a crossword in under 30 seconds

B.U.G.

ROLO

TOPS

CAPTAIN T-REX

DIPPY

STEG

SCIENTIST

FIRST COMMANDER

NAVIGATOR

MECHANIC

For Arthur J. H. Cherrington

First published 2016 by Macmillan Children's Books
an imprint of Pan Macmillan,
20 New Wharf Road, London N1 9RR
Associated companies throughout the world

www.panmacmillan.com

ISBN: 978–1–5098–1318–6

Text & Illustrations copyright © Ben Mantle 2016

1 3 5 7 9 8 6 4 2

A CIP catalogue record for this book is available from the British Library.

Printed in China

DINOSTARS
AND THE
CACKLING CAVE CREATURE

by Ben Mantle

MACMILLAN CHILDREN'S BOOKS

The Dinopod touched down in a huge rocky crater.
"I can't believe we're exploring the ruins of Flammas!"
squealed Rolo excitedly.
"We'll have to be quick," said Captain T-Rex. "This volcano
could erupt at any moment."

"Did you know," said Rolo, "the Eructans lived here for thousands of years? Then one day, they just left!"

"I'm not surprised," said Steg fanning himself. "It's so hot!"
"Oh, I don't know," said Rolo. "Once you get used to the heat, it really isn't that . . .

"LOOK OUT, B.U.G!" shouted Captain T-Rex, dodging a flurry of arrows.

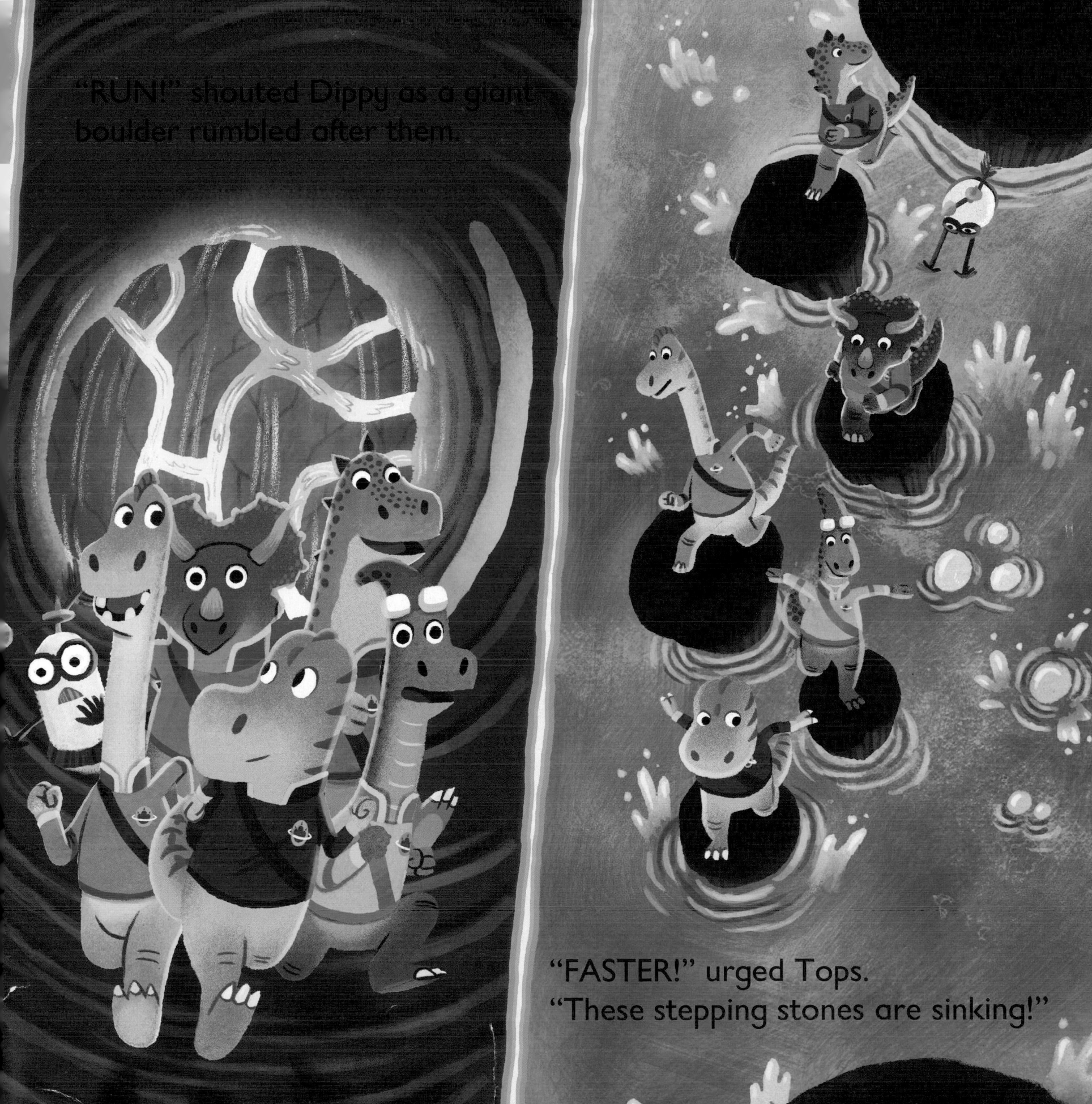

"RUN!" shouted Dippy as a giant boulder rumbled after them.

"FASTER!" urged Tops.
"These stepping stones are sinking!"

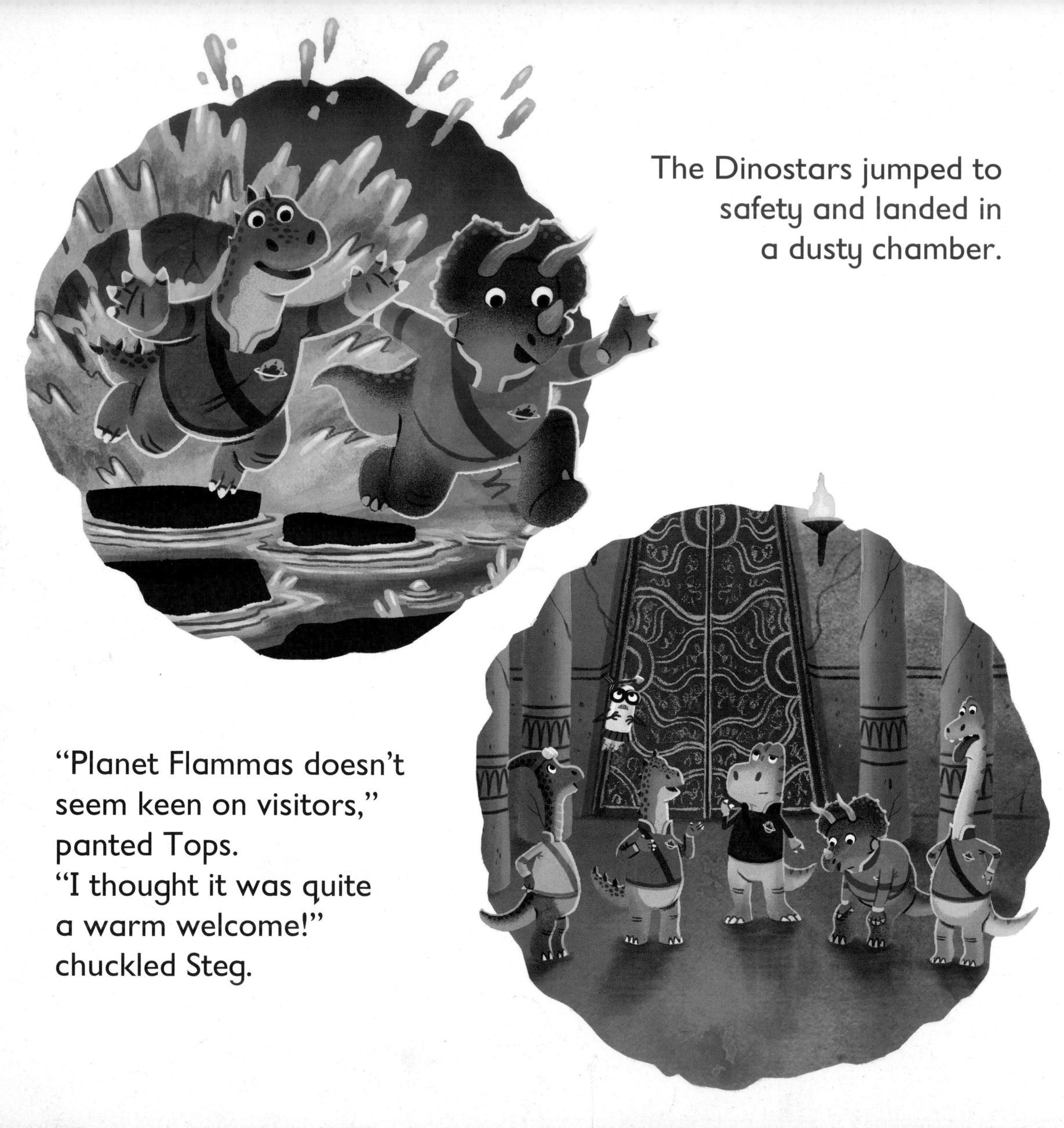

The Dinostars jumped to safety and landed in a dusty chamber.

"Planet Flammas doesn't seem keen on visitors," panted Tops.
"I thought it was quite a warm welcome!" chuckled Steg.

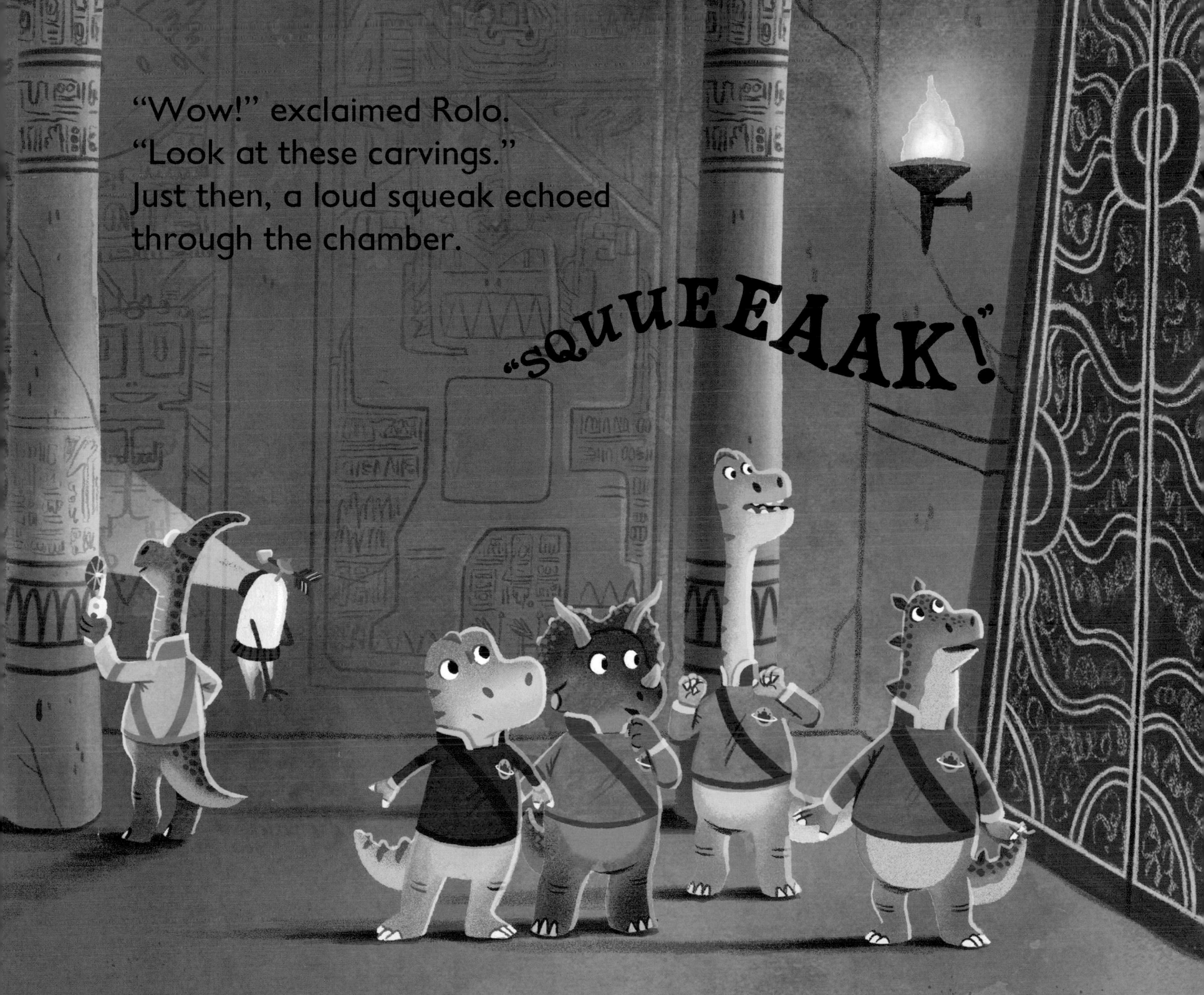

"Wow!" exclaimed Rolo.
"Look at these carvings."
Just then, a loud squeak echoed
through the chamber.

"SQUUEEAAK!"

"I thought there was no one else here?" said Dippy.
"That sound came from the next room," said Captain T-Rex.
"Rolo, you stay here and we'll take a look."

The Dinostars pushed open the heavy
doors and entered an enormous hall.
"What's that?" whispered Dippy,
pointing to the top of the steps.

A tiny creature blinked at them
and opened its arms wide.
"I think it wants a hug," said Tops.

As she reached out towards the creature . . .

it touched her nose and Tops began to tingle.

As quick as a flash, the creature bounced from Captain T-Rex to Dippy to Steg.

The Dinostars began to shrink smaller and smaller . . .

while the creature grew bigger and bigger, transforming into a . . .

gigantic MONSTER!

"ROOOOAAAA

It towered above the Dinostars
who had shrunk into baby Dino-tots!
The monster's bellowing ROAR
echoed throughout the cave.

Meanwhile, Rolo and B.U.G. were investigating the carvings. "It seems a ship crashed here carrying a mysterious creature that made the Eructans leave," said Rolo. "Those booby traps weren't trying to keep us out — they're keeping the creature in!"

AAARRR!"

"B.U.G., did you hear that?" said Rolo.
"I think the Dinostars are in trouble!"

They raced into the next chamber. But it was too late! The huge monster was closing in on them.

"STOP!" screamed Rolo, but the baby captain was already climbing onto its giant foot.

The monster growled . . .

then began to laugh.

The laugh turned into a loud cackle.

Suddenly the monster started to shrink . . .

while Captain T-Rex grew back to his normal size.

"Thank goodness," said Rolo handing him baby Dippy.
"Let's get back to the Dinopod while the monster isn't looking!"

"What happened?"
asked a very confused
Captain T-Rex.

"You just met a Muto from Planet Venetus,"
replied Rolo. "When it touches another species, the
friendly creature turns into a monster and changes
them into a baby. It seems the only way to reverse
the effects is to make the monster laugh."

The planet began to thunder and shake. "The volcano is starting to erupt!" shouted Captain T-Rex. We must get the Dinostars back to normal and leave this place."

"Don't worry," said Rolo. "I think I have an idea. But we'll need more of these arrows."

Rolo crept back to the ruins where the monster was lurking.

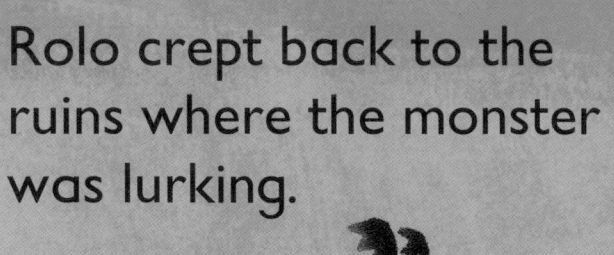

"I'm ready," she whispered to Captain T-Rex over the radio.

"OVER HERE!" she shouted.

The monster growled and bounded after her.

As it reached out to grab her . . .

Rolo shouted, "NOW!"

At that moment, Captain T-Rex dropped
a huge net onto the monster.

"TICKLE TIME!" shouted Rolo.
And the baby Dinostars jumped on
with the feathery arrows in hand.

The creature cackled with delight and started to shrink . . .

just as the Dinostars grew back to normal.

The volcano started to
rumble and spit.
"Let's go!" ordered Captain T-Rex.
"We can't leave him here,"
said Rolo pointing at the tiny Muto.

"You're right," said Captain T-Rex. "Dinostars, the Muto
needs our help."
"Hand me those arrows," said Steg. "I know who can help.
He's brave and got to work."

Moments later, Steg returned with a new invention. "Ta-dah!" he said. "It's a tickle hat to stop the Muto from getting into any more trouble while we take it home to its planet."

The Dinostars fired up the Dinopod. It blasted into Space with seconds to spare before the volcano erupted.

Before long they touched down on Planet Venetus and reunited the Muto with its family.
"Good work, Dinostars," said Captain T-Rex.

"Hee-hee!"

"Phew!" sighed Rolo, as they waved goodbye. "Now, let's explore Space!"
"Great idea!" said Steg. "I just hope we never see another Muto again."

ROLO'S SPACE FACTS

VOLCANOES

- Volcanoes are openings in a planet's surface. When they are active they can release ash, poisonous gases and magma.

- Magma is a form of hot liquid rock that lives underneath the surface of a planet. When magma comes out of a volcano it is called lava.

- Planet Earth is not the only place where volcanoes are found. Scientists have also found evidence of volcanoes on planets Venus and Mercury, and on the Moon.

- The biggest known volcano in our solar system can be found on Mars. Its name is *Olympus Mons* and it is approximately two and a half times as tall as Earth's Mount Everest is above sea level.

- Volcanoes can also be found at the bottom of oceans and under icecaps.